BEN'S SNOW SONG

A Winter Picnic

Story
HAZEL HUTCHINS

Illustrations
LISA SMITH

Warm Winter Wishes to Camrose Public Library!

Annick Press
Toronto

Third Printing, January 1991

Annick Press Ltd.

Annick Press gratefully acknowledges the support of the Canada
Council and the Ontario Arts Council.

Canadian Cataloguing in Publication Data

Hutchins, H.J. (Hazel J.)
　Ben's snow song

ISBN 0-920303-91-9 (bound)　ISBN 0-920303-90-0 (pbk.)

I. Smith, Lisa.　II. Title.

PS8565.U72B46　1987　jC811′.54　C87-094095-3
PZ8.3.H87Be　1987

Distributed in Canada and the U.S.A. by:
Firefly Books Ltd.
250 Sparks Avenue
Willowdale, Ontario　M2H 2S4

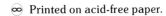 Printed on acid-free paper.

Printed and bound in Canada by
D.W. Friesen and Sons Ltd., Altona, Manitoba

To my family

The Snow is calling.
   In the back pack –
   dry pants
   extra mitts
   woollen scarves
   down vest
   hot chocolate!
   oranges
   hot dogs
   buns
   carrot sticks
   cheese and crackers
   cups

Get dressed
   undershirt, T-shirt, sweater
   long underwear, pants, snowpants
   little socks, bigger socks, biggest socks
   boots
   coat
   little mitts
   bigger mitts
   Leanna and Wil are ready too

Into the truck
     skis
     poles
     sled
     Dad's back pack
     Mom's back pack
     Wil, Leanna, me, Dad, and...
                                   ....Mom

Drive past the neighbours
    past the school
    across main street
    over the creek
    along the snowy road
    Here we are - everyone out

    Wax time - I can help!
    Wil and Leanna have short skis
    Dad and Mom have long skis
    The sled is for me - climb in

S *ki!*

Shhsskree, shhsskree, shhsskree, shhsskree
Sound of skis
Zee-zee-zee   Zee-zee-zee
Sound of chickadees

Sunlight, shadow, sunlight, shadow
Cold and quiet, world of snow
Top the hill
And down we go
Wheeeeeeeeeeeeeeeeeeee
(I never fall down.)

Sunlight, shadow, sunlight, shadow
Cold and quiet, world of snow
On and on
And on we go
Until . . . . .

LUNCH TIME!

Snap, snap
Gather kindling
Crack, crack
Axe on wood
Build a fire inside the shelter
When will someone get the food?

Out of the back pack –
    cups
    cheese and crackers
    carrot sticks
    buns
    hot dogs
    oranges
    Hot Chocolate
    and ginger bread men! (where were they hiding?)

    Cook the hot dogs
    Smell the fire
    Warm within the world of snow

Wil and Leanna
    Up the hill
    Down the hill
    Up the hill
    Down the hill
    All around so cold and bright.
    Warm my feet on Mommy's tummy
    Feed the grey jays
    Time to go

    Full tummy
    Warm hands
    Warm feet
    Cold nose

    Cold nose! Hey! Cold nose!

Full tummy
    Warm hands
    Warm feet
    Warm nose
    Song of skis
    Shhsskree, shhssskree, shhsskree, shhsskree
    Sunlight, shadow, sunlight, shadow,
    Cold and quiet, world of snow

    Sleep

Other titles by the author:
THE THREE AND MANY WISHES OF JASON REID
ANASTASIA MORNINGSTAR AND THE CRYSTAL BUTTERFLY
LEANNA BUILDS A GENIE TRAP